At the Palace Gates

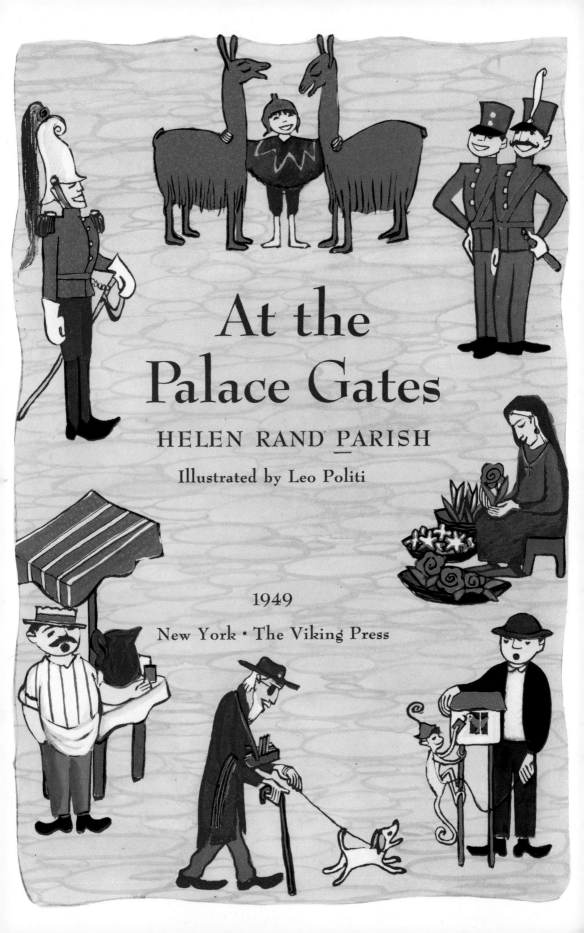

At the Palace Gates

HELEN RAND PARISH

Illustrated by Leo Politi

1949

New York · The Viking Press

SET IN BERNHARD MODERN BOLD AND GRANJON TYPES

AND LITHOGRAPHED IN THE UNITED STATES OF AMERICA

BY AFFILIATED LITHOGRAPHERS INC.

For Lito

Table of Contents

At the Palace Gates

I. The Chase

Paco had never been chased before. Many times he had run away, from boss-man after boss-man—one after another, in his native town on the road to Juliaca. He had been running away all his life as far as he could remember; that was because he was an orphan with no father, and no mother, and no family, and no real home at all. But now he was being chased for dear life, sure enough. And of all places, in Lima, the great capital of Peru, which Paco thought was probably the largest city in the world, and certainly the most wonderful.

The pavement felt hot under his bare toes. But it was good running: smooth, worn cobbles, flat asphalt, slick trolley-car tracks—much easier going than the crags and boulders back in Juliaca. His brown legs flew faster and faster. He only wished he were not so conspicuous in the big city in his dress of a little hillbilly Indian. In and out of the crowds he ran. People looked up to call "hillbilly" after him as he crashed into their sidewalk-tables and overturned their tea and jellies. He darted in front of taxicab wheels and leaped over sidewalk-carts like a mountain goat: a frightened little boy, not more than nine years old, his thin arms flailing out from his blanketlike poncho, his bronze face staring at the world in terror from under an incredible cap. It was a brilliant red-and-green knitted sort of bonnet with a peak on top, long ear-flaps, and a design of letters worked all around by somebody who could not read— Λ∀S∀B DESEbI —a flamboyant, ill-fitting thing that made him a perfect target for his pursuers.

Every now and then Paco would stop in his tracks, excitement getting the better of his terror. And he would look back, a grin playing over his mouth, black eyes flashing, at the two policemen chasing him. His curiosity was really stronger than his fear. And then he would streak on at top speed, losing himself in the crowd.

This was the way he had seen the wild vicuña flee from the hunters across the mountain-plateau of the Andes—the great Peruvian puna around the village where he was born. He had watched them so often, the little royal animals, the rarest and loveliest of all wild things, holding their tiny camel-like heads proudly, stretching out their thin hind legs, loping off into the distance like great golden-brown hares. And then stopping from time to time to look back at the hunters, with their overpowering, fatal curiosity.

Paco shouldn't have turned back that last time. They were gaining on him. Two policemen, and a queue of urchins at their heels, and even a man shouting "Stop thief, stop thief!" although Paco hadn't stolen anything. As a matter of fact, he hadn't done anything wrong at all. He was just running away from the Public Welfare—the orphanage people.

It had all happened about an hour back, just after he and his last boss-man, Don Pepe, had come into the city. Into the city of Lima at last, after months for Paco of traveling on foot with one boss-man after another across half of Peru. He had seen more country than he could remember; and more towns and villages than he could count; but never anything like this immense and wonderful metropolis. Don Pepe never had either; he was just an old man with hides to sell, not even a hillbilly Indian like Paco. Don Pepe was not quick on his feet at all, and that was why he had walked right into the truck carrying Donofrio Ice-creams.

Paco did not feel so very badly about the accident. Don Pepe was not much hurt, and enjoyed being fussed over by such a crowd of people, and having the police come and the big shiny white ambulance. He told Paco the Donofrio Ice-cream people would have to pay him money, and he was going to be very comfortable in the fine new Government hospital. Paco, he said, would probably be "gathered in"—rescued—by the Public Welfare Orphanage. Paco didn't want to be "gathered in"—rescued—by anybody. He knew all about the Public Welfare. They had come past it that very morning, on the way into the city. It was an awful-looking place. Great forbidding high walls of gray cement, and huge yards without a blade of grass in them, and a monstrous big building with little tiny windows. And rows of little plain-faced orphans out for a walk, with their dark skins and their school-aprons and their black stockings and their hair all cut alike. Paco could just imagine what it would be like to be shut up at the Public Welfare. Worse than being in the jail with barred windows that he saw once in Arequipa. Almost as bad as the cages they shut wild animals in, after hunters from his native hills caught them with their bolas,

the leather thongs, with three stones attached, that curled round
the animals' legs and tripped them.

So when Don Pepe had said Public Welfare, that was enough
for Paco. He had always been an orphan, as far as he knew, and
nobody had ever shut him up. And nobody was ever going to,
especially not the Public Welfare. He had let out a yell, leaped
through the air, and started to run headlong down the first street
he came to, like the wild mountain creature he was. Down street
after street he had plunged, down narrow Lima thoroughfares
with overhanging glassed-in balconies. Past bright shop windows
with silver bowls and lace doilies and starry-eyed mamma dolls.
Through an open place with a great sign—*Cine Metro*—in letters
big enough for even Paco to read as he raced past. On and on and
on, like the vicuña in the chase.

But after a half-hour, the policemen were gaining on him, and
in a moment he would have to give up because he could go no
farther. Paco was at bay, like an animal. He darted around one
last corner, and stood panting—a little Indian boy lost in the big
city of Lima, in his bare feet and his short poncho and his out-
rageous red-and-green knitted cap. Where to hide? Right ahead
he saw some stone steps leading up, an open door with wooden
panels—a church, just the place! He hesitated for a moment on
the threshold, then flung himself inside, into the dark and the
safety and the air that was fresh and cool like the wind of his native
puna. Paco would not have known the word for it, but he had
found sanctuary.

II. The Plaza de Armas

Paco stood quite still for a long time in the darkness. Nothing was moving inside the church. Outside, he fancied he could make out footsteps coming up the stairs, going away again. Then silence. Cautiously he stole back to the door and peered out: not a policeman in sight. Paco shook himself with relief and stepped out into the sunshine.

Before his eyes stretched the most amazing sight you could imagine. He would have thought it was a fairy tale—that is, if he had ever read any. It was a great huge plaza, a public square ten times as big as the one he had seen in Arequipa, all full of sunlight and noise and omnibuses, and sumptuous big buildings all around, and in the middle a park-place with grass and a fountain, and more people than Paco thought there were in the whole world.

The grandest part was the buildings, like the one on whose steps Paco was standing. From the size of it he guessed it must be a cathedral, not a church. Craning his neck far back, he could look up at its great stone front, with two gilded towers that went up and

18

up forever, and vultures circling in the air around them. And right next to it was another fine building with long enclosed balconies of brown wood jutting out from the second story—the residence of His Grace the Archbishop of Lima, although Paco did not know it.

Paco let out a low whistle, tucked his hands under his poncho, and started down the steps and into the crowd with the best swagger he could manage. The chase was over, the policemen were gone, and there was nothing to run from any more. He walked slowly, elbowing the passers-by. Nobody called him hillbilly here; nobody so much as looked at him, there were so many people. Some were even country Indians like himself, from all parts of Peru, right in with the city folks. But mostly they were grand gentlemen with canes, and ladies with high-heeled shoes and fur-pieces, and then raggedy men with woolen neck-scarves, and mulattoes, and Chinese, and swarms of bootblacks doing a thriving business right on the sidewalk.

Without quite knowing how, Paco had moved along with the crowd, and now found himself walking along another side of the plaza. Not along, that is, but under. For great old arches of peeling stone held up a roof over the sidewalk here. These passageways were called arcades, Paco knew. He had seen something like them in Arequipa. Except that the arcades in Arequipa were sleepy and quiet, like the main street back in Juliaca, but here it was like something in a dream. It was all life and movement and wonderful shops where you could buy marvels if you had money to spend.

Paco stopped in an open doorway where a sign said *Café León,* and joined a little knot of people who were gazing in. Oh, wonder of wonders! Inside, over the heads of people eating, was a screen with moving pictures that talked and everything. Paco had heard of such magic, but he had never beheld it before. And here in Lima it was to be seen free, just by looking through a door. For a while he stood there, but as he could not understand a word—the pictures were talking some strange language, not even Spanish— he moved out again toward the middle of the square.

It was hotter here in the park-place than under the shadowy arcades. People were eating their lunch on the wooden benches around the fountain, and throwing crumbs to the birds that pecked on the sidewalk. Paco was hungry too, and dug under his poncho for his precious moneybag that was knitted red-and-green exactly like his cap. It was quite full of hard-earned copper coins, and a few silver ones too, from many months of footsore travel and cuff-ings. He had never spent a cent, because the boss-man had always had to feed him. But now Paco was alone—a man himself—and had to spend his own money. He would have to be very careful of it.

Paco began by driving a thrifty bargain for a green alligator pear. And then, before he knew it, he was practically swindled. At least, he felt he should not have given his five-cent piece to the dancing monkey. But Paco had never had his fortune told before, and the man said this was the Monkey of Good Fortune, who could tell just what the future held. He was a rather dirty gray monkey who climbed up to a little wooden house on stilts and took out a paper for Paco. There were glass windows in the house too, and some birds flying in and out with colored sticks that had to do with your fortune. But Paco could not understand any of it, and when he looked at the paper that the monkey had given him, it was in the wrong kind of letters—the small ones that Paco had never learned how to read. After he had puzzled over it for some time,

he thought to ask the man what it said. But the man and the monkey and the little house had all gone, and there was only a photographer taking pictures and an old lady selling lottery tickets.

The sunshine had gone away too, and clouds were making shadows over the plaza. Paco looked around at all the strange faces and shivered. He was still hungry, and the alligator pear had not tasted very good. But he was afraid to buy anything else, and prudently tucked the useless fortune-paper into his moneybag. At this rate, he would spend all his coppers and get nothing for them. Evidently, this wonderful city was no place for a poor ignorant little hillbilly Indian like him, and he had better be on his way. He had better go back to the country and find himself another boss-man, and stay clear of all these wonderful things.

Paco was hanging his head and dragging his feet as he crossed over to the far side of the plaza, past the parked automobiles, up onto the sidewalk. For a fleeting moment he couldn't help feeling excited again at the sight of still another building, handsomer than anything he had yet seen. But he only shook his head at it sadly; these things were not for him.

Slowly he walked along by the iron grillwork, looking in at what could only be some great palace. All the other buildings— the Cathedral, the arcades, the splendid new structures that said *City Hall* and *Union Club*—were nothing, nothing compared to this. This Palace was longer and bigger and more impressive and more beautiful than anything in the whole world. It was made of square blocks of light stone, and in front of it were four-globed street lamps and great grilled gates. And right in front of the gates, pacing up and down on the sidewalk, were the two most gigantic and marvelous human beings Paco had ever laid eyes on. He would very much have liked to touch them: the two Palace guards in their red and white and gold uniforms and glistening casques with the manes of black horsehair waving in the wind.

But instead he ducked past their legs and slunk forlornly around the corner, his nose pressed to the grillwork, his little thin figure flattened against the Palace wall as though this could make him invisible. He was going to get away from here as fast as possible. He didn't belong in the city of Lima, but out on the free cold puna where he could run with the vicuñas that were wilder than himself.

Paco had even started to run a few steps, when suddenly he stopped in his tracks as though something had struck him. His heart stood still; the perspiration broke out on his thin little bronze face as he pressed it against the iron grille of the Palace and uttered a low cry. Paco could not believe what he saw. There, nibbling daintily on the green smooth-shorn grass, was the last thing he had ever expected to see in the city. Vicuñas, a pair of live vicuñas from his own mountains—graceful reddish-brown creatures looking right at Paco with their big moist eyes.

III. The Vicuñas

THE LARGER of the two vicuñas was taking a few steps in Paco's direction, lifting its elegant little feet high. It was a small brown creature like a baby camel—not more than three feet tall, its long neck arched, two curious tufts of white hair hanging down between its forelegs like an apron. Paco opened his eyes wide. He had never seen any vicuñas so tame as these. Without waiting for a moment, he tore off one of the red tassels from his woolen cap: no vicuña could resist red, he knew, and that was the best color to lure them with. And at the same time he dug into one of his many hidden pockets and reached out a handful of dried maize. They would probably like to eat that.

Holding his breath, Paco thrust an open palm through the grilled bars, the red woolly tassel temptingly laid among the grains of corn. And, without moving, he waited. It was not for long. The vicuña took a few more slow steps, then dashed forward to seize corn and tassel and all with its cleft mouth, and like a brown flash was loping off again across the lawn. But not before Paco, who was just as quick, had brushed the back of his hand against the softest, silkiest coat in the world.

25

The fleece—that was why people hunted the vicuña so cruelly, even though the Government tried to put a stop to it. The famous fleece of the vicuña that had always been the rarest and costliest thing in the Andes. Paco had often heard the old men of his village tell how, in the long-ago days before the white men came, when the great Inca had ruled over Peru, no one was allowed to kill the vicuña or wear a coat of its skin. No one but the royal Inca himself, who hunted it every four years for his own pleasure, and set free most of the animals he caught.

Paco guessed that explained it, why there should be vicuñas here in the city. This great Palace must be the house of the Government—of the Government which still protected the vicuña as in the days of the Indians. Perhaps some great gentleman lived here—sort of an Inca—and these were his own vicuñas that he had caught and kept for himself. They were quite young animals, no more than five years old, Paco would judge. And very tame. They had both stopped eating now, long enough to look at him with lively interest from a distance. Paco dug out another handful of corn and threw it between the bars; and the animals, bolder now, came quite close to eat it, working their white-marked jaws with obvious enjoyment.

Paco supposed that he, in his hillbilly clothes, looked just as familiar to them as they did to him. Vicuñas were such inquisitive animals anyway. They always dashed as close as they dared to the Indians who crossed the puna with pack mules, and even to the railroad tracks. And besides, he himself had spent most of his life running after vicuñas.

He had chased them every time he ran away from a boss-man, not hunting them but playing as they did across the great open puna. For whole days, as a very small boy, he used to follow them, as they grazed on the coarse yellow scrub grass of the barren table-land. And then he would climb up after them on the craggy sides of Mount Chachani, up under the glacier and the line of perpetual snow—leaping as they did from boulder to boulder and across mountain cataracts. Always they would be above his head, nibbling at moss and lichens on the edge of the precipices, starting away as he came near. But he would see them closer up in the sum-mertime, when the scant grass of the puna grew parched and dry. Then the vicuñas, with Paco after them, would go down into the valley, where the little Indian boy would lie on his back all day on the hill-slopes blue with lupin, while the animals fed on the lush grass below.

Once, Paco had even come upon a hurt vicuña, lying tumbled in a hollow by a stunted tree. At first he thought it was dead, because you never saw vicuñas lying down or even sitting. But he found that it only had a thorn in one of its soft toe-pads. The little wild creature let him take it out without a struggle and even gave his sleeve a playful nip of thanks. But as soon as the thorn was out, it ran off limping and disappeared from sight.

That was the very closest he had been to a vicuña—until now. But these two city vicuñas who belonged to the Government stayed even closer. Paco had thrown in every bit of his corn, and the two animals were almost at his feet, nibbling away without the slightest trace of fear. He could even hear them breathing, and he could have reached out his hand to touch them—except that he didn't want to frighten them off.

Paco turned slowly away. The shadows were lengthening across the sidewalk, and he must be on the move if he meant to be out

in the country before dark. But now he felt a little sad at leaving the city, now that he had found two mute friends in it. He had hardly taken a step, however, when he heard a sound he had heard only once before in his life—once high up on the slopes of Mount Misti, above Arequipa. It was the rare cry of the vicuña, soft and strange, something between the neighing of a horse and the belling of a deer.

Paco wheeled about. The two animals were looking at him fixedly, almost as though they were trying to talk. Was it more corn they wanted? Had this been a special treat for them? As though to explain that his pockets were empty, Paco thrust an empty hand through the grilles. And then, before he knew it, the littler of the two vicuñas had rushed up and nipped at his woolen sleeve, a playful little nip of affection like the wounded animal had given him long ago. The two vicuñas were right at the grille, their coats shining golden-brown in the sunlight, pleading with their big soft eyes. Pleading with him, in the wordless language of dumb animals, not to go away. The little hillbilly Indian knelt down on the city sidewalk, putting both hands through the bars to pat two velvety noses. He was not going back to the country, after all. He would find some way to stay here in Lima, near to the vicuñas he loved.

IV. The Bootblack

WILD animals, when they live amid dangers, take on what is known as protective coloring. The deer has spots like the speckled sunlight on the foliage where he hides. The butterfly looks brown and wrinkled like one of the old dead leaves on the branch where it sits. The field-mouse is gray like the earth and straw where she scampers. In this way, Nature protects all wild things so that they cannot be seen by their enemies.

This is what happened to Paco when he decided to stay in the great city of Lima and make a new life near the vicuñas of the Palace. In barely a week he had shed all the distinguishing marks of his hillbilly origin. The poncho, the moneybag, the outlandish red-and-green cap—all were gone, hidden away in a safe bundle. Now, nobody could pick him out from the other little urchins of the Plaza de Armas—for that was the name of the great square that had taken his breath away. Paco had become one of the bootblacks who daily shined the shoes of grand gentlemen on the broad sidewalk in front of the Government Palace.

To look at him at work, you would think he had been born and

30

brought up on the streets of Lima. He wore a shirt that had been white when he bought it, only now it was streaked over the stomach with all the hues of black and brown and tan and oxblood where he wiped his hands from the shoe polish. His dark breeches ended off above the knee, and were neatly held up by a single suspender. On the back of his head was a rakish little visored cap, such as schoolboys wear. As for his legs and feet, they were still bare, and considerably dirtier than when he first came into the city.

Setting up in business had not been easy. During the first two days he had spent the entire contents of the precious moneybag— all but one silver piece which was now in his "pocket bank," a secondhand leather coin purse that was slowly filling up with new coppers. Apart from his city clothes, he had had to buy a shoeshine-box, also secondhand, with wooden lids that opened up at each side of the handle, and a splendid assortment of rags, brushes, bottles, and waxes. These he had soon learned to use, for he was much more skillful with his hands than the city boys—having had a try, in his day, at basket-making and weaving and even the shaping of pottery.

Any day now he was to be seen—bright and early after the morning fog had lifted—at his accustomed place by the corner of the Palace grille. Most of the time he would be hard at work, kneeling on the sidewalk with a gentleman's foot on his knee, his little brown fingers flying back and forth over the shining leather and stopping only when he rubbed vigorously with his long sleeve —a system he had found much more efficient than the use of the rags and brushes. He gave, as he was fond of shouting at the top of his voice, the best shoeshine in the Plaza de Armas for "only one half-dime"—five cents.

Of course it was not all work for Paco. There was play, too, with the other bootblacks. Play of a rather rough sort, in which the little Indian's favorite sport was tormenting the police that had chased him that first day in Lima.

Every time a small, brown-faced policeman would come in sight, somewhat stooped in his dark uniform with revolver and white shoulder-belt, the boys would drop their work and gang up. And, like so many monkeys, they would scramble up into the niche on the corner wing of the Palace — with Paco always the first one up, as he was the best climber and runner in the square. Then, from their safe perch, they would hang out to shout down:

"Huairuru, huairuru!
"Beanie, beanie!
"Little dried up bea-nie!"

The helpless policeman would shake his fist and shout back insults in his turn; but as he could not stand there all day losing his dignity, he would soon have to move on.

But there were other sports among the bootblacks in which Paco could not share. The city urchins had no love for animals and would cruelly throw stones at the unfortunate dogs and horses that ventured past. Paco, however, loved all animals, from the tame pigs and chickens who used to come right into the mud houses of his native village, and the mules and little donkeys by whose warm sides he had slept on his travels across Peru, to the wild animals that had been his childhood playfellows on the puna.

Every morning, before setting up in business, he would bring the day's ration of corn to his friends, the two vicuñas of the Palace. They knew him well, and waited for him at the grille, and let him pat their silky coats through the bars. Paco held long conversations with them—in which he did all the talking, about his adventures and the places and people he had seen—while the two animals looked at him with their dainty little heads cocked to one side as though they understood every word.

Sometimes, when he had come very early, there was even time to run races. Paco would toss his cap in the air and dash clear down the block of the side street; and the vicuñas, streaking along the lawn, would pass him halfway and wait at the end of the course with a very foolish look of accomplishment on their camel-like faces.

At noon, Paco would share part of his lunch with them, to the derision of the other boys—who dared not laugh very loudly, however, lest the little hillbilly retaliate by promptly blacking an eye. And at night, before he went home, Paco never failed to say "Until tomorrow" to the vicuñas through the bars.

His "apartment" was only a niche in one of the old buildings—a wonderful niche protected by a convenient pillar from the prying eyes of the police. Here he had his cache: the rolled-up bundle of country clothes that served him for a pillow, and a collection of theatrical posters that he had slyly ripped from building-walls. These were of paper, and covered him better at night than the warmest blanket could have done.

Often, however, he would go home of an evening with one of his grown-up friends. For here, again, Paco was entirely different from the other bootblacks, who had no tolerance for adults any more than for animals. The little Indian had seen a lot of the world, considered himself already a man, and (except for size) found no difference between children and grownups. So it came that he was on intimate terms with a half-dozen of the picturesque vendors who had movable stands and booths in the Plaza—sometimes under the arcades, sometimes in the open sunshine, sometimes behind the Palace in the cobbled streets under the bridge.

One who fed Paco many good dinners was Don Feliciano, the lunchstand merchant, whose stock-in-trade was food and who had plenty of it. Evenings he would take the little boy to his house for a feed, prepared by his wife, of hot rice, meat tidbits broiled on a spit, and curds-and-whey. And in the daytime, Don Feliciano would occasionally treat Paco from the good things displayed under his awning, paper cups of pineapple-water from the big green glass jar, and an assortment of delicious Peruvian sweets: coconut candy, caramels, taffy, molasses peanut-brittle, and little doves made out of almond paste.

Then there was the fortuneteller man—he of the Monkey of Good Fortune to whom Paco had given his first five-cent piece in Lima. They had become fast friends, and the man had read him the fortune-paper, which said: "Seek no farther; your destiny is here." He even allowed Paco—alone of all the urchins in the Plaza—to play with the dirty little gray monkey, which used to sit and chatter on the bootblack's shoulder with one hairy arm affectionately around his neck.

His two very special friends, however, were Don Tiburcio the blind man, and old Señora Domitila who sold flowers. Don Tiburcio wore black glasses over his sightless eyes, and had a very intelligent white Spitz dog which guided him on a leash. He had a large tin tray hung around his neck by a ribbon, and dealt in hairpins, needles, packages of Gillette razor blades, folded papers of powder and rouge to be rubbed on the face, naphthalene moth-balls, tape measures, and combs. Paco had led him home on his arm many evenings, with the Spitz dog frisking beside them, glad to be free of his leash. And Don Tiburcio had given the bootblack one of his choicest ten-cent combs—and taught him the use of it.

Paco always carried his comb prominently displayed in the breast pocket of his blouse, and employed it on all important occasions. And one of these was whenever he went home with Señora

Domitila, the old flower-woman, who had many grandchildren
of her own and had the peculiar obsession (Paco thought) of wash-
ing them constantly. She washed Paco as well, called him "little

rascal-rogue," and said that he was leading an aimless existence as a bootblack in the Plaza de Armas and ought to give some meaning to his life by at least going to church on Sundays.

V. Francisco Pizarro

ONE BEAUTIFUL Sunday morning, when the shoeshining business had been unusually good, Paco decided to take Señora Domitila's advice. The Plaza was in holiday dress—ladies and gentlemen in their best clothes promenading and going up the steps of the Cathedral, and even the birds singing gaily as they splashed in the fountain. Paco thought that he, too, had better make himself presentable, and ducked his head under the spray of the fountain as he had done many a time in the mountain streams. Then he wiped his face on his sleeve, combed his wet hair down very neatly, tucked his shoeshine-box under his arm, and scampered across the street and up the Cathedral stairs where Señora Domitila was crying her wares.

The old lady, a shawl over her head, was sitting among her baskets of violets, wired gardenias, and artificial flowers made of cloth. *"Garden, Garden!"* she called out. "Just smell how sweet, Miss!" She gave Paco a kiss for his good impulse, tucked a handsome artificial flower through the buttonhole of his shirt, and speeded him on his way into the Cathedral.

Paco had not been inside since that fateful day he had hidden here from the police, and was much impressed by the size of the Cathedral, and the lights up in front, and the music—although he could not see very much over the heads of all the people. What most struck his fancy during the service, however, was a smiling little boy about his own age who came trotting down the aisle wearing a long red dress with a short lace jacket, and rattling a

38

wooden collection-box impishly in his two hands. Paco put some
money in as he saw other people do, and gave the box a loud shake
for good measure. Whereupon he and the lively "little friar," or
altar boy—for that is what the child in the red dress was—both
burst out giggling and were promptly shushed by the devout
worshipers all around.

After the service was over, Paco hung around in the empty
church in the hope that his new acquaintance would come out
again. He was not disappointed, for the little personage in the red
dress soon appeared (he had taken off his lace jacket), rushed up
to Paco, and stood open-mouthed, showing a place where a front
tooth was missing.

They made friends on the spot, and after Paco had exhibited his
shoeshine equipment the "little friar" countered by offering to
exhibit the mummy that was the pride of the Cathedral. Paco had
seen dead animals on the puna, mummified by the cold wind—and
so was a little surprised to find that this mummy was a man. An
exceedingly long man, who lay in a glass case on a great marble
box so high that you had to stand on tiptoe to look at him. You
could hardly see the face at all, everything was so dark, but you
knew it was there anyway. Paco was frightened and thrilled at the
same time. And, trembling, he led his little friend out toward the
warm sunshine of the steps, inquiring, with a voice that did not
sound like his own: Who might the mummy be?

The "little friar" spread his red skirts, sat down on the top step,
and started a game of penny-pitching before he answered. The
mummy, of course, was the real body of Don Francisco Pizarro,
same as him yonder on the horse; everybody knew that. Paco had
not known it. And he looked in wonderment at the great statue

that the "little friar" pointed out. He had never paid much attention to it before, but now he saw that it was an enormous man on a horse who dominated the raised terrace of the Cathedral and looked out over the Plaza as if the whole thing belonged to him. The horse was just ready to start, with a front foot lifted and a visor over its nose. And the stone man sitting astride it had a sword in his hand and a jutting beard—and on his head a plumed helmet that looked to Paco for all the world like the casques of the Palace guard.

Paco went on pitching pennies mechanically, without taking his eyes from the statue. He was not even ashamed to ask questions about the man on the horse, and the "little friar"—as talkative as Paco himself—was glad to answer. Don Francisco Pizarro, he said, had not been a particularly good man, but still he was the first Governor and Captain-General of all Peru. That was more than four hundred years ago, when Peru was most of South America. He had placed the cornerstone of this very Cathedral, and had laid out the Plaza de Armas. And over there—where the Government Palace was now—he had had his fine mansion, with a fig tree that he had planted himself growing under the window. The tree was still standing today—though everything else was gone—and you could see it just by looking into the garden of the Palace. As for the mummy, why, that was all that was left of his body after they killed him. For Don Francisco Pizarro had been murdered. . . . Which was a mad way to do, said the little friar, who went to school and knew whereof he spoke. Suppose you have a Government which is not particularly good—he smoothed down his skirts—all right, you talk, you hold meetings, and you vote in a new Government. . . .

But now for the story. It had happened on a Sunday morning long ago, right after High Mass at the Cathedral. Don Francisco had been warned of a plot, and so he stayed home from church. But his enemies—they were called the Men of Almagro—went across the Plaza to his house, and broke into the courtyard with drawn swords, shouting: "Death to the tyrant!" Some friends who were eating dinner with him fled by the back door. All the regular guard deserted, and even the special guard failed to bolt the door of the antechamber as his master ordered. Pizarro was left to face his assassins without his armor, and alone—alone except for two young page boys who stayed faithfully at his side, the only heroes in this whole bad business. He drew his sword—he was a famous swordsman—but there were too many against him. Both of the heroic page boys were killed, and the Governor fell at last. He made a cross on the floor with his own blood and kissed it as he lay dying. And then his friends had come, and brought his body over here to the Cathedral, where it had been ever since.

Paco drew in his breath with amazement. He had never heard a story so wonderful and so terrible—and true, besides. He stood up and removed his cap respectfully before the statue of Governor Don Francisco Pizarro. His friend Señora Domitila was right, indeed, when she said that his was an aimless existence. What was he but a little "rascal-rogue" of a bootblack, in this great Plaza de Armas where so many fearful and heroic deeds had been done!

VI. The Farewell

AND NOW Paco was not even going to be a bootblack any more. For since that sunny day when he had gone to the Cathedral and learned about Don Francisco Pizarro, his whole little world had crumbled about his ears. The most dreadful, the most unthinkable, thing had happened to him.

Paco listened to all the bells of Lima booming out the Angelus at once, and thought it was the saddest sound he had ever heard. He covered his face with his hands, where he sat huddled in his "apartment," surrounded by his torn posters that flapped in the wind. All day long he had been hiding here, only waiting for the twilight in order to steal out without being noticed. He was in trouble again, real trouble. And this time not with any old beanie of a policeman. This time it was with the Palace guard—with those wonderful giants in the uniforms and shiny casques. They had turned out to be his enemies after all.

It was all on account of the vicuñas. Early Monday morning he had been feeding them as usual, when the head guard had come up behind and seized him by the ear. For some time, he said, they had been keeping an eye on Paco and his suspicious carryings-on.

They had seen him bouncing on the back springs of the State carriage when it was parked out front. They had watched him clamber into the niches and swing on the gates. And especially they had noticed that he spent half his time leaning through the grilles after the animals. Nobody was allowed to hang around the Palace this way; there was a guard to see to that. If he was caught just once more, he would be turned over to the police. And no sprinting off on those fast legs, either. Straight into the police wagon he would go, and down to the station house for questioning. To be sure, if he proved to be just a harmless loafer without a proper home, he would not be punished. Just "gathered in"—rescued—by the Public Welfare Orphanage.

The Public Welfare! So that was what it came back to, after all these months in Lima. After several days of trying to stay clear of the Palace, Paco had reached a heartbreaking decision. He was going away forever. He had sold his city clothes and his shoeshine-box to another boy, and this night—this very minute—he was leaving Lima never to return.

The bells had finished booming. It was late enough now, and starting to grow dark already. With a heavy heart, Paco crept out of his "apartment" into the half-empty Plaza. He was wearing his old hillbilly clothes, which had grown quite small for him. The red-and-green cap looked more ridiculous than ever, with the flaps no longer covering his ears. And he felt uncomfortable in the short poncho, with his cumbersome knitted moneybag tied at his waist. He had even parted with his "pocket bank," his city coin purse, and had kept only a few keepsakes: his comb, his artificial flower, and the piece of folded paper with his fortune. Every word of it was false, that stuff about "Seek no farther; your destiny is here."

The fading afternoon was overcast, with the leaden winter sky low above it as Paco walked slowly—for the last time—across the Plaza de Armas. The air was thick and chill with the heavy watery mist that in Lima is called rain. Drops of it spread on the steps of the Cathedral, stood out like perspiration on the statue of Don Francisco Pizarro. The arcades were deserted, with the wetness streaking down the arches and the corrugated tin shutters of the closed shops. Even the spray of the fountain was gray and color-less, like the sky, half invisible in the misty air. A horse clop-clopped on a side street, and a single taxicab honked and skidded

by on the damp pavement. Paco's feet were cold and wet, and he was shivering under his poncho. As he crossed over to the corner where he had been a happy and carefree bootblack, the Palace looked more beautiful to him than ever—so grand and white and long in the twilight, with the globes of the street lights shining yellow on the railing. And he was leaving all this fairyland to go back to a little mud village on the road between Juliaca and Cuzco. A little mud-and-stone village where a wooden ox-plow was a curiosity, and where he would be cuffed around by boss-man after boss-man and grow up to be nothing but an ordinary hillbilly Indian.

A rolling of drums brought Paco back to himself. It was time for the changing of the guard, and he hid behind a lamp post to view this magnificent sight for one last time. The posted guards were marching away from their places by the two gates, and by the double marble staircase inside the courtyard, which Paco knew was the front door of the great Government-gentleman who lived inside the Palace. As they marched off, others marched on to take their places, with rifles—or were they swords?—held in their white-gloved hands. The lamplight shone on their broad chests and great shoulders in white tunics with gold braid, on their fine long legs in red trousers, on their resplendent silver-colored casques with the gallant black horsehair waving behind. The drums were still rolling, and the guards were marching stiffly by—intent on their own solemn splendor, with no time to notice a little Indian boy lurking in the shadows.

Unobserved, Paco stole around the corner to say good-by to his beloved vicuñas.

It was darker here by the grilles. The lights were out on this side of the Palace, and the two animals nuzzled at Paco through the bars with odd little frightened noises. They were trembling under their silky coats just as he trembled under his poncho, and Paco knew—as surely as though they had told him—that some-thing was wrong. Something in there, in the gardens, was dread-fully wrong.

The little Indian peered inside, his sharp eyes growing ac-customed to the darkness, every mountain-trained sense alert for some danger. He could see shadows, a group of men, moving far back in the garden. And through the low roll of the drums, and the sound of the near-by Rímac River under its bridge, he thought

he could hear voices. Yes, they were voices—talking in whispers that only sharp ears like Paco's could have made out.

What were they saying? "Strike the blow . . . Midnight . . . Death to the tyrant!" Paco's black hair was almost standing on end under his cap, and an icy sensation crept down his spine. "Death to the tyrant!" Why, those were the words of the "little friar" when he told of the murder of Don Francisco Pizarro. These must be bad men—the Men of Almagro—Paco had no other name for them. They must be planning to murder the great, good Government-gentleman who lived in the Palace and kept the vicuñas. Just as four hundred years ago other bad men had planned to kill Don Francisco Pizarro.

And what could Paco do? He was helpless. He couldn't call the police, he couldn't call the guard. They all distrusted him; they wouldn't even listen to him, but would only drag him off to the Public Welfare. There must be someone, somewhere, to whom he could go for help. Before his brain had made the decision, Paco's fleet legs had started to run back across the Plaza through the wet night—back toward the only street where there were lights and life and people at this hour, the Jirón de la Unión. There he would find his friends the street vendors at their trade—the sweetmeat-man, and the flower-woman, the blind man with the Spitz dog, and he of the fortune-house and the monkey and the lying little papers that said: "Your destiny is here."

VII. The Fig Tree

THE vendors had all thought Paco was out of his head when he found them and rounded them up in the Jirón de la Unión. But the panic in his little brown face, and the strange earnest sight of him dressed for going away in his hillbilly clothes, and the tone of urgency in his shrill voice, had made them come anyway. They had stolen back through the night, across the empty Plaza, to the side of the Palace, Don Tiburcio in the lead with his white Spitz dog, moving with the silence of the blind. And after him the fortune-man, with his little house on one shoulder and the monkey on the other, and even the birds silent in their cage. Then Don Feliciano of the good food, holding Paco by the hand. And finally poor old Señora Domitila, shuffling along in her felt slippers, her shawl wrapped around her head and her arms still full of flowers.

Sure enough, there were the men inside the garden, just as Paco

51

had said. Sure enough, anyone could see they were up to mischief,
slinking around under the balconies. The blind man, whose ears

were sharper even than Paco's, could hear words that were not good, and said that the men were armed. And then somebody had made a noise, and the scuffle had broken out all at once—with out-cries and throwing of stones through the grilles. The animals had got into the garden somehow, the monkey and the dog, one over and one under the bars. Paco had climbed over after them, and the good-luck birds had flown in from their overturned house. And as for those who stayed outside, they were shouting at the tops of their lungs, and throwing in not only stones from the street but everything they carried: flowers and candy and hard naph-thalene-balls, and tape measures and combs—all pelting in at once on the Men of Almagro. Pelting in while the dog bit and the monkey scratched and the birds pecked and Paco let fly with his hard little fists and feet. Even the vicuñas took part in the fight, letting out their weird cries and spitting with deadly aim right in the eyes of the assassins.

The whole thing could not have lasted more than a few minutes —though it seemed longer to Paco, what with the shouting, and the rocks that he dodged, and the shots going off all around. And then the deafening noise had brought the whole guard running in force from the front of the Palace, drums still rolling.

Before Paco knew it, everything was over. Lights had been turned on in the garden, and the place was swarming with guards. Through the lifting smoke he could see everybody being led away: the Men of Almagro in the elegant dark suits that grand folk wear to parties—looking very unelegant indeed with their coats torn, and their hair in their eyes, and their wrists handcuffed. And his friends the vendors, their belongings smashed and strewn on the sidewalk, surrounded by guards as they moved away all talking at once. Even the animals were being rounded up and taken into custody, except the vicuñas, that were nowhere to be seen. Outside the grilles, a crowd of spectators had collected to watch and were looking in at Paco, who was all alone in the center of the garden.

He stood quite still, rubbing a bruise on his cheek, and let himself be taken without even kicking the guard. It would have been no use anyway, as he was the biggest of them all—the head guard who had told Paco to go away. The guard had recognized him, too; you could tell by the questions he asked.

Now Paco was really caught, and there was no escaping. A great heavy hand had clamped down on his shoulder; one of the guards was walking in front of him, and one in back, and several by his sides, as they went across the garden. Paco felt funny and calm inside and looked around at all these things he knew he would never see again. There were curvy Moorish tiles of every color, and palm trees no bigger than a boy, and little clipped hedges, and dozens

of potted plants, and all sorts of paths in pretty patterns. It smelled
so nice here in the garden, with the wetness and everything, and
suddenly Paco felt all tired and achy inside of him. He would have
liked to forget everything, to lie down by one of the tiled benches,
and go to sleep and never wake up again. His face was swelling,
and he guessed he had a black eye, and his jaw was sore.

For a moment, as he walked, he thought he was going to be
sick. And then he saw the fig tree. An old, old fig tree that was just
a gnarled trunk and a single branch, and that stood in a place by
itself as though it was important. It could only be the one the
"little friar" had told him about—the fig tree that Don Francisco
Pizarro had planted with his own hand. Paco did not feel sick any
more. He was remembering about that other fight, long ago, when
everything had come out so differently. When the guard had fled,
and the Men of Almagro had stormed the Palace, and the Governor and the page boys had lain dying in their own blood. The
little Indian held his head high as he marched through the smoke
of the garden. He didn't know what would happen to him now,
but things had turned out pretty well after all. And it *had* been a
beautiful fight.

VIII. Señor Presidente

Paco supposed it was the Public Welfare for him now. The guards had marched him around to the front courtyard, and at sight of the police wagon waiting outside, his momentary elation vanished and the awful sick feeling came back over him. But they weren't taking him out through the gates, after all. The squadron had turned sharply left and had started up the brightly lit marble front steps of the Government Palace itself. The globes were shining out all the way up the railing, round and yellow like so many moons, and over the door Paco saw the shield of Peru: a tree, and a curved horn, and a camel-like animal that he took to be a vicuña.

When they actually led him through the front door, Paco won-
dered if all this could be a dream. It was so bright in here that he
could not stop blinking and rubbing his eyes, and he could hear
the drums still rolling in his ears though he knew they had stopped
long ago. The marble floor was like ice under his toes, and over-
head great chandeliers blazed down on his red-and-green cap with
a light that was brighter than the sun itself. With a full escort of
six guards, he padded on and on in his bare feet through the
mighty length of the Palace, down halls without end, up a staircase as long as clear across the Plaza. And all the while the head
guard steered him by the shoulder and said never a word.

For once in his life, Paco said nothing either. He thought he had
quite lost the power of speech, and his poor legs felt so weak under
him he was sure he could never run again. At last they stopped in
front of a huge carved door, where another guard stood with a
drawn sword. A word the "little friar" had used flashed across
Paco's mind: antechamber. He had said, "The special guard at the
door of the antechamber." Could this be it? The door was being
opened, and Paco was led in by the head guard, who spoke to him
for the first time.

"The Señor Presidente will see you now," he said in a voice
that was strangely gentle. Then he saluted and backed out, closing
the door behind him.

Paco was left alone, in a great tapestry-hung room, with vast
expanses of shiny floor stretching out before him. Down at the far
end were two great damask armchairs, and in one of them sat a
kind-looking gray-haired gentleman beckoning with an uplifted
forefinger. That must be the great Government-gentleman himself, the Señor Presidente who owned the vicuñas. Paco trotted

obediently over, and looked up, half blinded by the light of a candelabrum with crystal drops that stood on a golden post in the corner of the room. He looked up, and then down again, reddening in sudden embarrassment.

Paco knew instinctively that this was the moment for some gesture of respect, like the guard's salute. He felt that he, too, should do something for the Señor Presidente. He would have liked to fling himself on his knees and shine the great gentleman's shoes. But when he stole a glance at them, he saw that they needed no shining. They were the shiniest, glossiest, blackest patent-leather shoes that Paco had even seen. Timidly he let his eyes travel upward. The Señor Presidente was shining all over, like his shoes. The satin lapels of his black evening-suit gleamed; the white shirt-bosom shone dazzlingly. Across his chest glowed a broad ribbon in the red-white-and-red that Paco knew were the colors of the Peruvian flag that waved over the Palace. About his neck, on a long chain, hung a jeweled medal that sparkled like a million stars. Even his quiet face looked white and shining to Paco—the hair silvery gray, the lenses of the eyeglasses glistening over the bridge of his nose.

Decidedly, this gentleman did not need a shoeshine. And besides, Paco had sold his bootblack equipment anyway. Nervously he pulled off his cap, dug into a pocket for his comb, and hastily combed his hair. The artificial flower had fallen onto the floor, and the grimy paper that said: "Seek no farther; your destiny is here." Paco did not even bother to pick them up, for the Señor Presidente had begun to speak.

In a voice as kind and quiet as his face he was talking, and nice and slow too. First he asked Paco's name, and then he pointed to

the other armchair and said: "Sit down, Paco." Which the little Indian did clumsily, his cap held in his hand, and his short brown legs dangling over the rose-colored damask.

The Señor Presidente knew everything, he said. The guards had told him, and the blind man, and even the police. He knew all about Paco, and the Public Welfare, and the bootblacking. He knew how Paco came to feed the vicuñas every day. Above all, he knew that Paco was a hero and had routed the wicked men from the garden. Solemnly the Señor Presidente reached out and shook Paco by the hand.

"Thank you for saving my life," he said simply. It was not he himself, he explained, who thanked Paco. It was the Peruvian nation. Peru was a democracy, which meant that the President was chosen by the people and represented all of them and tried to do what was best for everybody. So if the President were killed, more would be lost than just the life of one man. It would have been a step backward for democracy, a triumph for violence and evil men.

Paco nodded. Somehow, in spite of the big words, he understood perfectly. But the Señor Presidente had not yet finished; he was talking about Paco himself. Peru, he said, did not wish her orphans and poor children to live in the streets. Paco would have to be "gathered in"—rescued. Paco bit his lip; this meant the Public Welfare for him, he was sure.

The Señor Presidente had stopped speaking and was ringing a bell-cord. And now the door had opened once more, and all six of the guard—Paco's escort—had come in and were standing at attention. Paco slid out of his chair and stood quaking before them. The Señor Presidente was leaning forward to ask a question.

"Would you like to stay and live with us here?" he said.

Paco could not believe his ears; he was not quite steady on his bare feet, and the whole room was swimming. Maybe it was a dream after all. But no, it was true. He was really being asked if he would like to stay at the Palace for good, and have the special duty of taking care of his own beloved vicuñas! And there was still more: the whole guard was offering to adopt him for his heroism. And when he grew up, he was to be one of them and wear the glorious uniform and the casque like Francisco Pizarro, and stand at the door of the President's antechamber. Only—the President had raised a forefinger to his eyeglasses—only he would have to wear shoes and go to school.

For a moment Paco thought of running away once more. Perhaps he did not really belong here at the Palace, after all; he was just a wild hillbilly Indian. And then he remembered that the vicuñas were wilder still, and yet they lived here very happily. Paco lifted a swollen face to the Señor Presidente, who was repeating his question:

"Would you like to stay and live with us here?"

"Yes, sir . . . yes, sir!" said Paco, his face crinkling into the old roguish grin. And then the young hero of so many adventures let the head guard pick him up in his great arms, where he closed both eyes and fell asleep almost at once, like any tired child.

The little orphan had found a home at last—inside the Palace gates.